FAST LANE

AR 2.0

Bristol Met LRC

R04580F4586

CW00840126

First published in 2008
by Franklin Watts

Text © Simon Allen and Deborah Smith 2008
Illustrations © John Charlesworth 2008
Cover design by Peter Scoulding

Franklin Watts
338 Euston Road
London NW1 3BH

Franklin Watts Australia
Level 17/207 Kent Street
Sydney, NSW 2000

The authors and illustrator have asserted their rights in accordance
with the Copyright, Designs and Patents Act, 1988.

All rights reserved. No part of this publication may be
reproduced, stored in a retrieval system, or transmitted
in any form or by any means, electronic, mechanical,
photocopy, recording or otherwise, without the prior
written permission of the copyright owner.

A CIP catalogue record for this book
is available from the British Library.

ISBN: 978 0 7496 7719 0

Printed in Great Britain

Franklin Watts is a division of Hachette Children's Books,
an Hachette Livre UK company.
www.hachettelivre.co.uk

The Hide

Spike T. Adams

Illustrated by John Charlesworth

BRISTOL METROPOLITAN ACADEMY
SNOWDON ROAD
FISHPONDS
BRISTOL
BS16 2HD

W
FRANKLIN WATTS
LONDON•SYDNEY

Chapter 1

"Keep running, Jono!" I shout.

Dale and his heavies are after us.

And Jono's lagging behind.

"I can't, Jase!" Jono gasps.

Jono and his big mouth.

He can never keep it shut.

OK, so I agree.

Dale's new haircut is lame.

But ya can't say it.

Not to his face!

"You two are dead!" Dale shouts.

We turn a corner.

Jono slumps against the wall.

"Come on!" I say.

I can't leave him.

Dale and his crew will mash him up!

"This way!" I hear Dale shout.

I look back.

Here he comes — Owen and Robbie behind him.

Dale sees me — and grins.

I turn to grab Jono...

But Jono's gone!

Done a runner — without me.

I can't believe it.

So it's three against one now...

"Where's fatboy?" Dale sneers.

"Don't worry. We'll get him later."

And he steps towards me.

I cane it out of there.

Dale goes to grab me — misses.

"Get him!" he yells.

The three of them storm after me again.

I sprint — fast as I can.

Past some kids in the corridor.

Slipping and sliding on the floor.

I race round into another corridor.

There's a door at the end.

It's locked!

No way out.

I back against the wall.

Breathing fast.

My fists ready.

"Ya can run, Jase!" calls Dale. "But ya can't hide!"

"That's what he thinks..." says a soft voice.

I feel a cool hand slide along my arm.

And turn to see...

...a dark, shadowy gap in the wall next to me!

The hand slides into mine.

It pulls me in.

And the gap closes.

Chapter 2

Behind the wall it's dark and dusty.

"Where did he go?" I hear Owen say.

"This door's locked."

"He's vanished!" says Robbie.

"Nobody just vanishes!" Dale snaps at them.

I hear him tap on the wall.

Hold my breath.

I think Dale is gonna find me.

But then he stops.

"Keep on looking," he orders.

I hear them stomp away.

"Safe now, Jase..." says a voice next to me.

My eyes get used to the dark.

I turn to see who saved me.

"Tasha!" I say. Shocked.

She used to be in my class.

But she ran away.

She nods and smiles.

I swallow hard.

She's close to me.

"Where are we, Tash?" I ask.

"It's called The Hide, Jase," she tells me.

BRISTOL METROPOLITAN ACADEMY
SNOWDON ROAD
FISHPONDS
BRISTOL
BS16 2HD

Tasha takes my hand again.

Hers is so soft and cool.

But it soon warms up in mine.

She makes me HOT.

"I can hear your heart beat," she says.

My face burns.

She leads me up some dusty old stairs.

Then along a narrow passage.

"When did ya come back?" I ask her.

"I never went away, Jase," she says.

I'm shocked.

"Ya been here — all this time?" I say.

"Doing what?"

She grins. "Just watching...and partying."

Tasha stops.

Puts an eye to one of the holes in the wall.

She giggles.

"Look at this!" she says.

I have a look.

And see Mr Carter and Miss Jones.

In the staff room – getting it on!

"Bwoy..." I say, shaking my head.

Tasha laughs.

"That's nothing," she says.

"You're going to see much more than that!"

We move on.

Up more stairs.

Along more passages.

And then I can hear giggles...

Running water...

Showers...

The girls' changing room!

"No way!" I shout.

"Shh! Keep it down," Tasha hisses.

I look through a spy hole.

You can see EVERYTHING.

Tasha pulls me away, laughing.

Chapter 3

Up the next stairs is a room.

There are others in there.

Kicking back, chilling out.

One of the guys comes over.

We touch fists.

"Welcome to The Hide, Jase," he says. "I'm Ed."

"Ed looks after us all," Tasha tells me.

I look over to the others.

One of them is bragging.

"Yeah, I coulda taken all three!" he says.

It's Jono.

I go over to him.

"Yo! Jase! Ya got here!" Jono says.

"How did *you* get here?" I ask him.

Jono points to another guy.

It's Tank!

Tank used to be in the year above us.

Until he got kicked out last year — for nicking stuff.

"Tank pulled me in," Jono tells me.

I nod at Tank.

Tank nods back.

Then I look at all the great stuff in the room.

Ipods, PSPs, clothes...

"Ya nick all this?" I ask.

Tank nods again.

Ed comes over with Tasha.

"Things get left in classrooms," he says.

"We take what we want."

He holds out his arms.

"Help yourself to any of it," he says.

"There's more where this came from."

Then he yawns. "Time for some rest," he says.

He turns to Tasha.

"You and Tank, show our new guys some fun."

Tasha nods.

She looks pleased.

And so do I.

Chapter 4

Tasha and Tank take us up into a narrow space.

We all crawl along.

"See where you are?" Tasha asks me.

I peer through a secret hatch in the floor.

We're above our classroom!

"Dale, Owen and Robbie are under me!" I tell Jono.

"Gob on them," says Tank.

"They won't see ya!"

Jono pushes me out of the way.

"I'll do it!" he says.

We all watch.

Jono gets up a good gob of spit.

Then lets it dribble down.

It lands right on Dale's head.

Result!

"What?" Dale says.

He reaches up. Finds the spit.

And then turns to Robbie.

"Ya little shite! Ya gobbed on me!"

Robbie shakes his head.

But too late — Dale punches him.

Owen starts to snigger.

So Dale turns and punches him too.

"Detention, Dale!" shouts Mr Carter.

We roll around laughing.

We make our way back to the den.

I'm still laughing.

Bwoy! Jono and me are having such a sick time.

Ed is back when we get there.

He smiles when he sees us.

Such white teeth.

They glint and gleam — even in the shadows.

Ed's got this big old silver cup in one hand.

And a bottle in the other.

It looks like red wine.

"Time for a drink…" he says.

The others cheer.

Now we're talking.

"Yo! Let's party!" Jono shouts.

Ed pours wine into the silver cup.

Passes it round.

It feels a bit weird.

Aren't there more glasses?

Jono doesn't care. He takes a swig.

He swallows.

The others cheer.

But then Jono's eyes widen.

"It tastes like..."

Then he barfs all over himself.

Everyone groans and leans away.

I shake my head.

Jono looks a right prick.

Tasha helps Jono to his feet.

"I'll take care of him," she tells Ed.

"Good girl, Tash," Ed says.

He gives her a wink.

I grit my teeth as they go off.

Jono and Tash — together.

How does he do it?

"Just take a sip, Jase," Ed says, handing me the cup.

I nod. But then a kid runs in.

"Fight!" he shouts.

And everyone jumps up.

I put the cup down.

Follow the others.

Chapter 5

We're over the changing room.

Dale is down there.

Robbie and Owen are hitting someone.

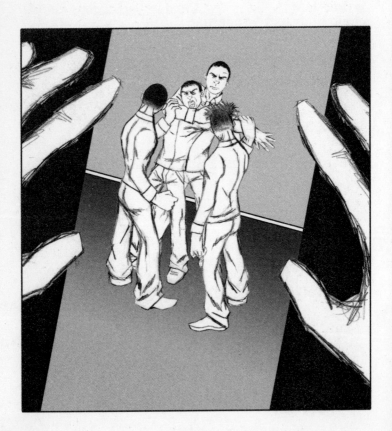

"Hit him harder," Dale orders.

So Robbie does.

"Get him out of here," Dale says.

So Owen slams him into the door. Out into the corridor.

Dale laughs. Spins Robbie and Owen some notes.

"Let's celebrate. I'll have a Super Hot 'n' Spicy pizza," he says. "And double garlic bread."

Robbie and Owen hurry off.

Dale goes over to the mirror.

Smiles at himself.

"He's so got it coming," I say.

Ed grins and nods. "He so has..."

A panel slides open.

Ed swoops down. Yanks Dale off his feet like he's a toy.

Then leaps back up to the ceiling — with Dale!

Dale is kicking and punching.

Ed pinches Dale's neck — he passes out.

Ed leads the way back to the den.

Carrying Dale, no trouble.

The others follow.

So do I — but what's going on?

How come Ed can do that stuff?

Jono and Tasha meet us.

All smiles.

Jono's eyes are all shiny now — like Tasha's.

And there's a mark on his neck.

"Is that a lovebite?" I hiss at him.

He just grins.

Ed takes Dale to the table.

Lays him out like a slab of meat.

He sits by Dale's neck.

"Let's drink!" he calls.

The others gather round.

"Great, I'm thirsty!" says Tasha.

Ed smiles — he's grown fangs.

And he sinks them into Dale's neck...

VAMPIRES.

They share Dale like a super-size shake.

Sucking his blood.

Tasha looks up.

Dale's blood drips from her chin.

"Come sit by me, Jono," she says.

I look at Jono.

He's got fangs too...

Tasha's lovebite...

...it's turned Jono vampire!

"NO!" I shout.

I try to pull Jono away — but he pushes me to the floor.

He sits down next to Tasha.

Smiles back at her.

And then bites into Dale's arm.

I shake my head.

Then edge to the door.

I've gotta get outta here!

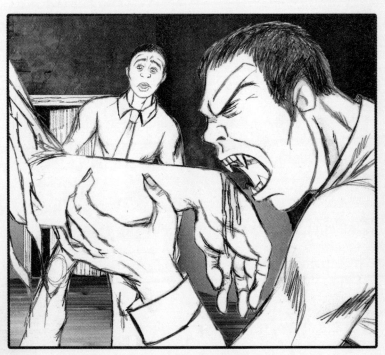

Chapter 6

I run down the stairs.

Along the passage.

There's gotta be a way out.

Left or right now?

I don't know — it's like a maze.

I bang on the walls. Shout for help.

Hope someone on the other side will hear.

Then I hear a roar from the den.

"FIND HIM!"

The vampires are coming to hunt me down.

I keep on running in the dark.

The vampires are close.

Footsteps and flapping wings.

And then...

I hear a voice from below.

"Where's Dale?"

Owen!

"Who cares? Let's eat it ourselves."

Robbie!

I must be above the changing room.

So there's a panel here — a way out!

I feel on the floor.

Find the panel.

Slide it open — and jump down.

Owen and Robbie just stare at me.

Mouths open — full of pizza and garlic bread.

"We have to run!" I shout.

Too late.

The vampires are here.

Ed, Tasha, Tank — and Jono — land in the room.

Tank blocks the door.

We're trapped.

Tasha comes over.

"Let me take care of you, Jase..." she says.

She runs ice-cold fingers along my neck.

Then reaches up to kiss me.

I shake my head and push her away.

"Ya fit, Tash," I say.

"But you're a blood-sucker."

Tasha shows her fangs.

"Your loss, Jase!" she hisses.

Then leaps up — out of the room.

"She can fly!" Owen yells.

"She's got fangs..." croaks Robbie.

"So have I," says Ed, smiling.

He comes for me...

I grab Owen's garlic bread.

Shove it right in Ed's mouth.

He staggers back, and then screams.

His open mouth is full of smoke and ashes.

Ed's lips are burned black.

His face begins to flake away.

"So the movies are right!" says Owen.

"Vampires don't like garlic!"

Chapter 7

Tank grabs Ed — back up to The Hide.

So now it's just Jono.

He licks his lips and looks at me hungrily.

Robbie grabs a piece of garlic bread.

Holds it up to Jono — like a gun.

Jono growls as Robbie comes at him.

"No, Robbie!" I shout. "Leave him alone!"

Jono turns to look at me.

"Ya still my friend, Jase..." he says.

"But I'm one of them now."

And he leaps back up to The Hide.

Someone else comes flying down.

We get ready.

This time he falls to the floor.

And then moans, "Urgghhh...."

It's Dale.

I look up – the panel to The Hide is closed.

"What happened to Dale?" asks Owen.

"He ain't one of them is he?" asks Robbie.

He pushes the garlic bread into Dale's mouth.

"Urgghhh...!" Dale says again. "It's gone cold!"

I shake my head.

He ain't no vampire.

Next day, people are looking for Jono.

"They say he's run away," Robbie tells me.

"That's what *we* should do," says Owen.

"Before they get *us*!" says Dale.

I shake my head.

"No," I say. "I've got a better plan..."

I open my bag to show some wooden stakes.

"Ya get what these are for?" I ask.

Robbie nods. "Bwoy! Ya well tooled up!"

"So what are we gonna do?" Owen asks me.

"Simple," I say.

I hand Dale a stake.

"We're going on a vampire hunt..."

Jon feels bad about Ricky.

Ricky's a geek. A loser.

He gets picked on all the time.

Then one day, up at the Outlook, Ricky is pushed way too far...

978 0 7496 7718 3

More titles by Spike T. Adams:

978 0 7496 7716 9

978 0 7496 7717 6

AINDERBY STEEPLE C.

Missio[n] Cancelled!

by Jem Packer
Illustrated by Emma Levey

OXFORD
UNIVERSITY PRESS

In this story ...

Pip and Kit run *Finders Squeakers* – a lost and found agency. They help return lost things to their owners.

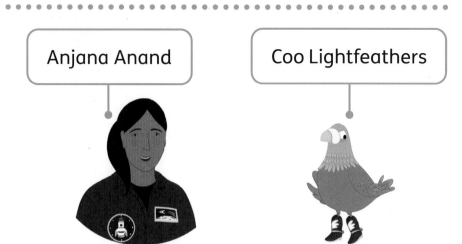

Chapter 1
10 minutes until take off ...

"Hurry up, Pip!" said Kit. "We need to be close to the front if we want a good view of the rocket."

"Coming!" replied Pip.

Pip and Kit squeezed through the huge crowd until they finally found a good spot.

Pip and Kit sat down. They had a great view of the giant rocket that was about to launch from the Tailton Space Centre.

"What a <u>scene</u>!" Pip said.

"I can't wait to see Anjana Anand blast off!" Kit replied. "She'll be the first astronaut to walk on Mars!"

Can you describe the <u>scene</u> in front of Pip and Kit? What might they see and hear?

Just then, there was an announcement.
"TAILTON, WE HAVE A PROBLEM!"

"What's going on?" said Pip.

"We are sorry, everybody," said the announcer.
"Anjana's space helmet has gone missing. She
can't go to Mars without it. THE MISSION
IS CANCELLED."

The crowd groaned with disappointment.

"This sounds like a job for *Finders Squeakers*!" Kit said.

"Yes, we need to find that helmet," agreed Pip. "First we need to get into the Tailton Space Centre ... and I know just how we're going to do it!"

Chapter 2
To the space centre!

Pip and Kit ran to the car park, where they'd left their motorbike. Pip got a large box from the sidecar.

"I've wanted to test this out for ages," Pip said, opening the box. She pulled out a strange machine that looked a bit like a metal rucksack. "This is my new jetpack!"

Pip strapped the jetpack on and pushed a button. The jetpack made a rumbling noise, and Pip hovered in the air.

"Is it safe?" asked Kit.

"Of course!" said Pip, grabbing Kit's paw. "At least ... I think SOOOOOOOOOOO!"

Pip and Kit shot into the air.

They flew over the tall safety fence towards the Tailton Space Centre building.

"Isn't this great?" Pip said, looking around in <u>amazement</u>. Kit just whimpered.

Suddenly, the jetpack spluttered. "Uh oh," Pip said. "I'm losing power!"

They plunged down. Pip steered through an open window into a huge pile of cardboard boxes.

Can you show the expression on Pip's face as she looks around in <u>amazement</u>? How might her expression change as the jetpack loses power?

Pip and Kit got shakily to their feet. Pip took the jetpack off and looked around.

They were in an enormous room filled with bits of machinery. "This must be where they build the rockets," Kit said.

Pip peered down a corridor. "Let's start our search for the helmet down there," she said.

Chapter 3
A familiar face

As they headed down the corridor they saw a strange-looking astronaut. The astronaut had wings and a beak, and looked very <u>familiar</u>.

"Coo Lightfeathers!" Pip said. "I should have known you'd have something to do with this. Where's the missing helmet?"

Does '<u>familiar</u>' mean that Pip and Kit have seen this astronaut before, or not? How do you think Pip felt when she recognized Coo?

"I don't know where the helmet is," Coo said. "But when I find it, I'll be the first pigeon in space. I'll be famous!"

"Not if we find it first!" cried Kit.

"You forget that I have an <u>advantage</u> over you," Coo said, taking off. "I can fly and that makes me faster!"

"He's right," puffed Kit as they raced after Coo. "He'll find the helmet first at this rate."

An <u>advantage</u> is something that is better than something else. What <u>advantages</u> might a cat have over a pigeon?

"I've got an idea," said Pip. She skidded to a stop. "Hey, Coo," she shouted. "They are interviewing for new astronauts back at the launch pad. There are TV cameras there!"

"TV cameras?" said Coo. He immediately turned and flew out of a window.

"That wasn't true," Pip said, "but it should give us some time to find the helmet!"

Chapter 4
The search

The first place Pip and Kit looked was in the astronauts' changing room. Rows of blue and orange suits hung on hooks.

"I can't see a helmet, but I think this looks good on me!" Kit said. He had climbed into one of the suits.

Pip grinned. "Let's keep looking," she said.

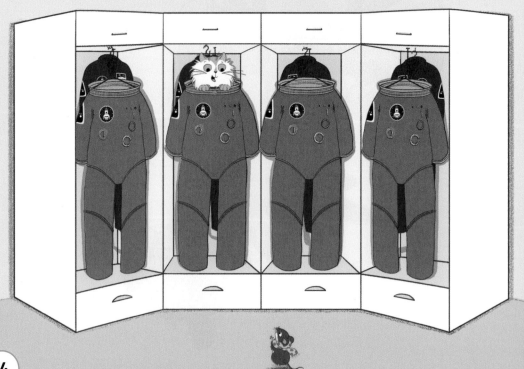

Next, they investigated the canteen. They looked under the tables and in the kitchen.

"No helmet here," said Pip.

Just then, there was the sound of footsteps.

"Is it Coo?" Pip whispered.

A man entered with a trolley. "No. It's a cleaner," replied Kit. "Let's go."

The next room was the zero-gravity room.

As Pip and Kit stepped into the room there was a humming noise, and they both floated up.

"Look at me!" Kit laughed as he tumbled through the air.

"Very impressive, Kit," said Pip, "but there are no helmets in here!"

Finally, they had a look around the control room. It was full of computers and large screens.

"No sign of the helmet here either," said Kit.

As they left, Pip noticed a fishbowl on a tall stand in the corridor outside. "Hmm, that's odd," she said. "It's empty."

Chapter 5
Intergalactic Goldie

Pip went up to the fishbowl. As she did so, she stepped in a puddle. "The floor is wet!" she said.

There was a sign on the stand. Kit picked Pip up so she could have a closer look.

The fish who lives in this fishbowl is called Intergalactic Goldie … the first fish to go into space!

"Where is Goldie now?" asked Pip. Then she spotted a trail of water on the floor.

Pip and Kit followed the water all the way to the cleaner's storeroom. They went in.

"There's another fishbowl here," said Pip. "Goldie's inside!"

"That isn't a fishbowl," said Kit. "It's ..."

"THE MISSING HELMET!" cried Pip. "The cleaner must have borrowed it to put Goldie in while he was cleaning the fishbowl."

"He must have forgotten all about Goldie in the excitement of the launch," added Kit. "We've got to get the helmet to Anjana."

"First we have to return Goldie to his proper bowl," said Pip.

Pip and Kit carefully carried the helmet and its contents across to the fishbowl.

"Let's pour him back in," said Kit. He heaved the helmet up and gently <u>released</u> Goldie back into his fishbowl.

"Well done, Kit!" said Pip. "Now to find Anjana!"

How do you think Goldie felt as he was <u>released</u> back into his fishbowl? Can you think of another way of saying '<u>released</u>'?

It didn't take Pip and Kit long to locate the astronaut. Anjana was in the changing room, searching for her helmet.

Pip and Kit placed the helmet by her locker. Then they hid.

"Look! My helmet," said Anjana. "That's strange. It's a little damp. I'll give it a quick dry, and then I will be ready to go to Mars!"

Later that day ...

"5 ... 4 ... 3 ... 2 ... 1 ... ," boomed the announcer.
"BLAST OFF!"

The crowd applauded wildly as the rocket took off.

Pip and Kit cheered. The only one who wasn't happy
was Coo ...

It's not <u>fair</u>!
You didn't wait
for me!

Coo doesn't think it's <u>fair</u> that the rocket is
taking off without him. Do you think it's <u>fair</u>?
Does he deserve to go to Mars?

Read and discuss

Read and talk about the following questions.

Page 4: Can you describe the <u>scene</u> that you can see in front of you at the moment?

Page 9: What was the last thing you watched in <u>amazement</u>? Why did it <u>amaze</u> you?

Page 11: Can you describe someone who is very <u>familiar</u> to you?

Page 12: Do you think it is unfair to have an <u>advantage</u> over someone in a race?

Page 21: What did Pip and Kit <u>release</u> into the fishbowl?

Page 23: Can you think of a time when you've said: "It isn't <u>fair</u>!" What was not <u>fair</u>?